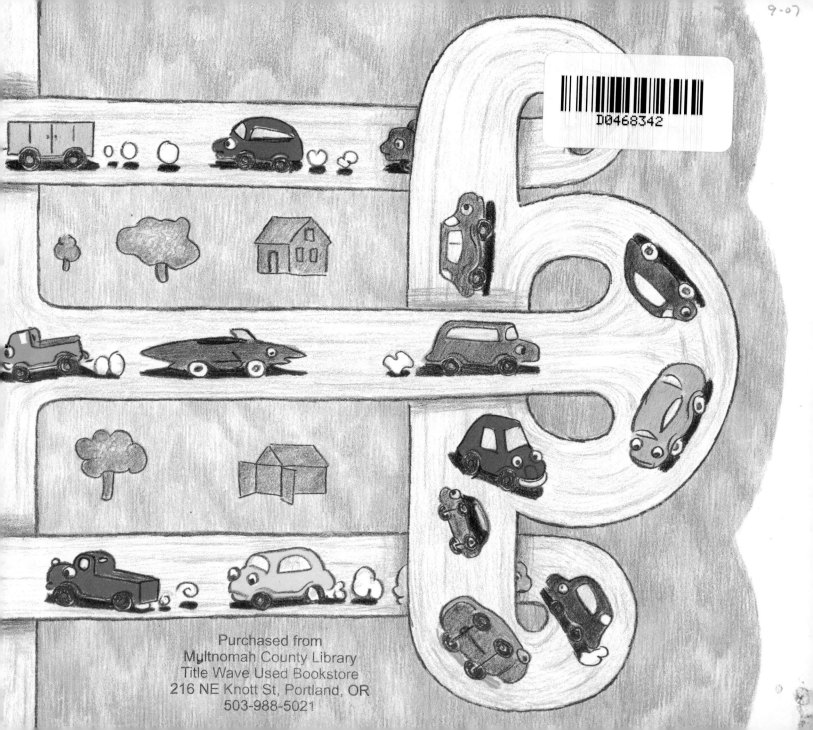

THE TWO CARS

Ingri & Edgar Parin d'Aulaire

THE NEW YORK REVIEW CHILDREN'S COLLECTION

New York

THIS IS A NEW YORK REVIEW BOOK
PUBLISHED BY THE NEW YORK REVIEW OF BOOKS

Published in the United States of America by
New York Review Books
1755 Broadway, New York, NY 10019
www.nyrb.com

Library of Congress Cataloging-in-Publication Data

d'Aulaire, Ingri, 1904–1980.
The two cars / written and illustrated by Ingri and Edgar Parin d'Aulaire.
p. cm. — (New York Review children's collection)
Summary: On a magic moonlit night, the sleek, shiny automatic new car and the
beat-up old car with many miles on its speedometer go for a drive to see which
car is the best.
ISBN-13: 978-1-59017-234-6 (alk. paper)
ISBN-10: 1-59017-234-5 (alk. paper)
[1. Automobiles—Fiction. 2. Fables.] I. d'Aulaire, Edgar Parin, 1898–1986.
II. Title.
PZ8.2.D275Tw 2007
[E]—dc22
2007002636

ISBN 978-1-59017-234-6

Cover design by Louise Fili Ltd.

This book is printed on acid-free paper.
Manufactured in China by P. Chan & Edward, Inc.

1 3 5 7 9 10 8 6 4 2

OTHER BOOKS BY INGRI AND EDGAR PARIN D'AULAIRE

D'Aulaires' Book of Animals

D'Aulaires' Book of Norse Myths

D'Aulaires' Book of Trolls

Once there were two cars who stood side by side in a neat garage with white walls and green trim.

On a magic moonlit night they began to talk.

"Look at me," said the one. "I am streamlined and new and glossy and green. My paint is hardly dry behind my fenders. My gearshift is automatic, my pickup is swift. I am the best car on the road."

The other car said, "I am no longer young. My red paint is chipped. My luster is gone. I am one hundred thousand miles old. But I am strong and willing to go at the touch of a toe. I am the best car on the road."

So they agreed to go for a drive to see who was the best car on the road.
The new green car was smooth and quick. He switched on his key and
flicked into gear. In the wink of an eye he disappeared around the bend.

The old red car was cold. He sputtered and coughed as he stepped on his starter, and all his old joints rattled and squeaked when he changed into gear. He went into first, into second and third, then he was off and rumbled down the road in pursuit of the new car.

On a long, steep hill he caught up, for the old car could change into low
while the new car lost speed.

On top of the hill they hit a big bump. Up bounced the old car and down again he came with a terrible bang. He was almost knocked out. But he did not lose control of himself. The new car lay down flat on his fine new springs and hugged the road.

The two cars whizzed around a sharp corner and came to a field where many small animals of the woods were playing in the moonlight.

"Honk, honk, you watch your step and I'll watch mine," honked the old car. Gently he shooed a small rabbit out of his way so as not to hurt

a single hair.

"Toot, toot, toot, shoo fly, make room for the fastest car on the road,"
shrilled the new car. Rabbits and squirrels jumped for their lives and a
turtle went tiddlywinks. And there was the new car, far ahead.

But a little way down the road there was a railroad crossing. Up the tracks the milk train was coming.

"AAAAOOOOUUUUT of my way!" came the wail of the train. It blinked its lights and rang its bell.

The new car slammed on his brakes and came to a screeching stop. It hurt him in his brand-new white-wall tires.

The long, heavy train rumbled by. First came the locomotive, then the coal car, then 25 cars loaded with milk. At last came the red caboose. And the wise old car had timed himself so well he came around the corner and dove across the tracks just after the caboose had passed. The new car stepped on the gas and whizzed off. Still, the old car was ahead.

The two cars came to a nice, flat stretch of road. They both drove along smoothly, not faster than allowed, but not slower either. Their motors liked the cool night air and purred like kittens.

After a while they came to a dreary place where there was a car dump. The old car looked down into the dump with sad eyes.

"Poor old Mrs. Plym," he said, "why did you have to go so fast

around that corner and get yourself all smashed up! And you, Miss Chevvy, young and pretty, you had to get yourself all tangled up with that old Ford! And you, Mr. Caddy, the proudest of us all, why did you beat that red light? There you are now, rusting to pieces." The old car had to slow down, for he felt a hot tear trickling down his crankcase. He didn't know whether it was water or oil.

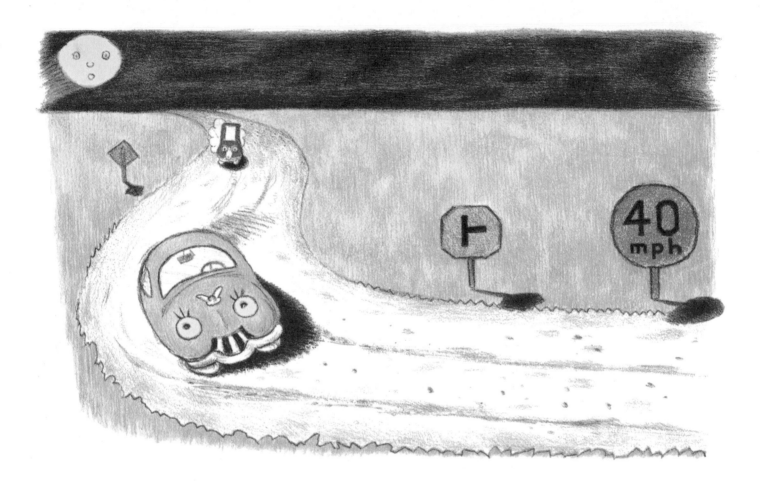

But the new car! He felt jauntier than ever when he saw the old wrecks. That could never happen to him. He stepped on the gas. Roadside signs flashed by. One said, NO PASSING, but he passed the old car. Another

said, 40 MILES AN HOUR, but he didn't care. He reached 50, 60, and
65. His pistons sang in unison. Life was nothing but fun.

Suddenly a harsh voice jolted him out of his happy thoughts.

"Pull over to the curb," a big fat policeman shouted.

"Oh, oh," said the new car to himself, "I forgot to watch through my mirror." Aloud he said meekly, "I am sorry, officer," and hoped this would soften his heart. But it did not.

"Where is the fire?" the policeman asked gruffly. "Let me see your license."

The new car felt very blue as he pulled the license out of the compartment.

"First offense, five-dollar fine. You had better watch out, next time it will be more," said the policeman. With that he turned around and smiled broadly at the old car who was just passing by at an even 40 miles an hour. No more, but no less either.

For once the new car was not so fast in his getaway. He looked back after the fat policeman and called loudly, but not so loud that he could hear it, "Officer, you have a flat!"

Then the new car set off in pursuit of the old car, who was far ahead by now. The new car almost caught up at a dangerous intersection, for there the old car had come to a full stop. He looked first to the left, then to the right. "Nobody here, nobody there, then I'll go," he said.

But as the new car wanted to cross, a half-ton pickup truck came

tearing down the crossroad. He acted as if he owned the roads.

"Toot, toot, I came first," said the new car politely.

"The right of way is mine," said the half-ton pickup truck.

"You think you are so great, you half-pint truck," said the new car.

"And you think you are so smart," said the truck, "I'll shove you."

Bang. He bumped right into the new, green car, but thank goodness he hit only the bumper. The new car heard a long S-C-R-A-T-C-H as the pickup truck shoved him out of the way and sped down the road. He jumped out to look at the damage. All he could see was a hairline scratch along his shiny new bumper. Still he was mad and wanted to

fight. But the truck was far away by now. So was the old red car.

Once more the new car set off in pursuit. But now he was careful. He went 40 miles an hour, no more, no less either. At an even clip he held the same speed, uphill and downhill and over flat stretches. But so did the old red car. The old red car was going to win. He had almost reached

the driveway when the policeman popped up in front of him and said "Stop!" The old car pulled over. He was surprised, for as far as he knew he had done nothing wrong. Meekly he fumbled around in his compartment until he found his license. The new car came closer and closer while the policeman looked at the license. He nodded his head and smiled a

broad smile, and just then the new car passed!

"Mister," he said, "I want to congratulate you on your safe and beautiful driving. Not too fast, not too slow, and careful around the corners. That's the kind of driving I like to see."

Out of the corner of his eye the old car saw the new car make a lovely turn up the driveway. He saw how he bent and turned his sleek green body and slid smoothly right into the garage. "Thank you, officer," he said humbly.

But it was a proud old car that drove up into the garage and parked himself nicely beside the new car. "You won the race, but not the praise. I still think I am the best car on the road. But you will be a fine car, too, when you get older," said the old car to the new car.

The moon went down and in the dark, dark night the two tired cars slept and slept.

INGRI MORTENSON and EDGAR PARIN D'AULAIRE met at art school in Munich in 1921. Edgar's father was a noted Italian portrait painter, his mother a Parisian. Ingri, the youngest of five children, traced her lineage back to the Viking kings.

The couple married in Norway, then moved to Paris. As Bohemian artists, they often talked about emigrating to America. "The enormous continent with all its possibilities and grandeur caught our imagination," Edgar later recalled.

A small payment from a bus accident provided the means. Edgar sailed alone to New York where he earned enough by illustrating books to buy passage for his wife. Once there, Ingri painted portraits and hosted modest dinner parties. The head librarian of the New York Public Library's juvenile department attended one of those. Why, she asked, didn't they create picture books for children?

The d'Aulaires published their first children's book in 1931. Next came three books steeped in the Scandinavian folklore of Ingri's childhood. Then the couple turned their talents to the history of their new country. The result was a series of beautifully illustrated books about American heroes, one of which, *Abraham Lincoln*, won the d'Aulaires the American Library Association's Caldecott Medal. Finally they turned to the realm of myths.

The d'Aulaires worked as a team on both art and text throughout their joint career. Originally, they used stone lithography for their illustrations. A single four-color illustration required four slabs of Bavarian limestone that weighed up to two hundred pounds apiece. The technique gave their illustrations an uncanny hand-drawn vibrancy. When, in the early 1960s, this process became too expensive, the d'Aulaires switched to acetate sheets which closely approximated the texture of lithographic stone.

In their nearly five-decade career, the d'Aulaires received high critical acclaim for their distinguished contributions to children's literature. They were working on a new book when Ingri died in 1980 at the age of seventy-five. Edgar continued working until he died in 1985 at the age of eighty-six.

TITLES IN THE NEW YORK REVIEW
CHILDREN'S COLLECTION

ESTHER AVERILL
Captains of the City Streets
The Hotel Cat
Jenny and the Cat Club
Jenny Goes to Sea
Jenny's Birthday Book
Jenny's Moonlight Adventure
The School for Cats

SHEILA BURNFORD
Bel Ria: Dog of War

DINO BUZZATI
The Bears' Famous Invasion of Sicily

INGRI AND EDGAR PARIN
D'AULAIRE
D'Aulaires' Book of Animals
D'Aulaires' Book of Norse Myths
D'Aulaires' Book of Trolls
The Two Cars

EILÍS DILLON
The Island of Horses
The Lost Island

ELEANOR FARJEON
The Little Bookroom

RUMER GODDEN
An Episode of Sparrows

LUCRETIA P. HALE
The Peterkin Papers

MUNRO LEAF AND ROBERT LAWSON
Wee Gillis

NORMAN LINDSAY
The Magic Pudding

ERIC LINKLATER
The Wind on the Moon

E. NESBIT
The House of Arden

BARBARA SLEIGH
Carbonel: The King of the Cats

T. H. WHITE
Mistress Masham's Repose

REINER ZIMNIK
The Bear and the People
The Crane